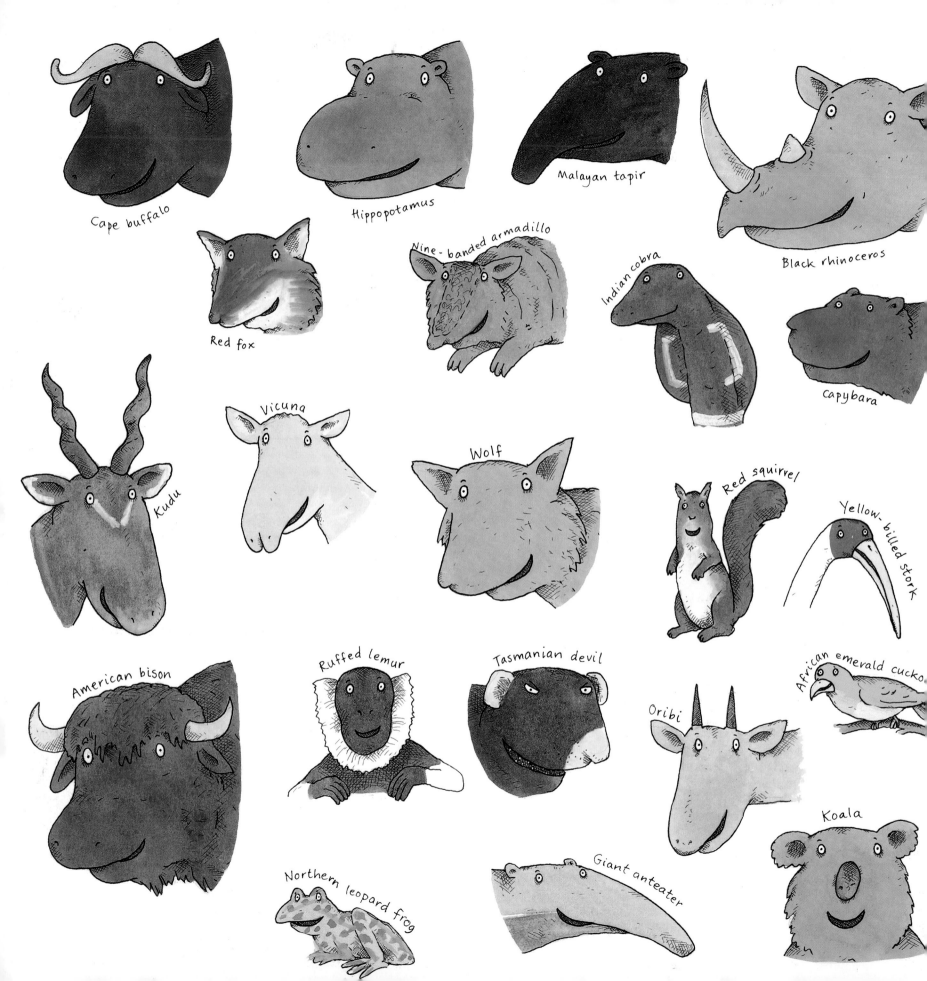

Cape buffalo

Hippopotamus

Malayan tapir

Black rhinoceros

Red fox

Nine-banded armadillo

Indian cobra

Capybara

Kudu

Vicuna

Wolf

Red squirrel

Yellow-billed stork

American bison

Ruffed lemur

Tasmanian devil

Oribi

African emerald cuckoo

Koala

Northern leopard frog

Giant anteater

Leopard

Proboscis monkey

Moufflon

Polar bear

Macaroni penguin

King penguin

Adelie penguin

Jackass penguin

Emperor penguin

Ring-tailed lemur

Otter

Moose

Meerkat

Northern elephant seal

Emerald tree boa

Golden eagle

Carrion crow

Great horned owl

Greater flamingo

Shoveler

Lappet-faced vulture

TWO BY TWO
BY TWO

Cape buffalo

Warthog

Lion

Red fox

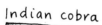
Indian cobra

Golden eagle

Dik-dik

Northern leopard frog

Indri

Alligator

Black rhinoceros

Reedbuck

Elephant

Brown bear

Brown hare

Lesser horseshoe bat

Two by Two by Two

by

Jonathan Allen

Moose

Coral snake

Orion
Children's Books

First published in Great Britain in 1994
by Orion Children's Books
a division of the Orion Publishing Group Ltd
Orion House
5 Upper St Martin's Lane
London WC2H 9EA

A catalogue record for this book
is available from the British Library
Printed in Italy

It all began when God told Noah that there was a terrible flood coming and that he must build a boat big enough to save himself, his family, and all the animals. By *all* of them he didn't mean every single one, just two of each kind, one male and one female.

So Noah and his three sons, Ham, Shem and Japhet built an enormous boat called the Ark.

When the rain started the animals came to the Ark in pairs, two by two… by two… by two… by two… by two…

They ran up and down the corridors
looking for their cabins.

There was room for everyone.

As soon as they were settled in, they began to make friends.

The bald eagles introduced themselves to an elephant. Some small birds chatted to a reindeer. The wood mice swapped stories with an alligator.

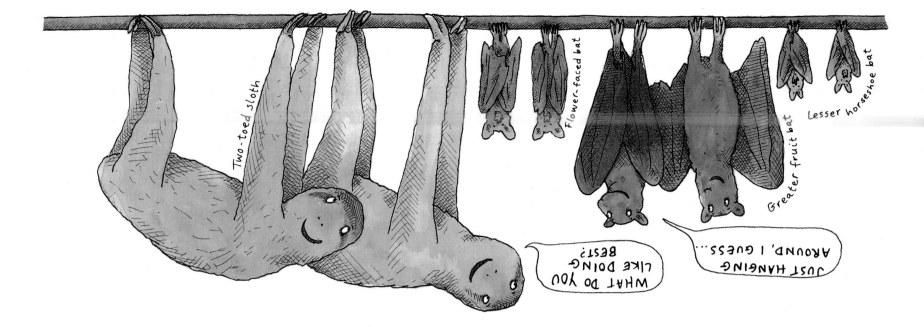

The sloths and bats joined the Upside Down Society.

The ducks and geese got to know the duck-billed platypus. They'd never seen anything like him! What kind of creature was he?

And in an isolated corner, the skunks and polecats founded the Smelly Society.

But not all the animals behaved so well. A wolf and a leopard thought a game of skittles would be a good idea, using penguins for skittles and armadillos for balls.

The spider monkeys tried playing darts with the kingfishers. Luckily the porcupine stepped in with a kind offer before any harm was done.

A pygmy hippopotamus had a swing on a handy piece of brightly coloured rope…

…and the chimpanzees set up a Fur and Hair Clinic, with hedgehogs as hairbrushes.

Things were getting out of hand. Noah had to have stern words with them all.

To keep them out of trouble, he organized some games. The soccer tournament was a great success, until the hippopotamus went in goal.

The rams, bears, Bengal tigers and bulls wanted a game of American football, but nobody else would play with them.

For the more adventurous types there was hang-gliding from the upper deck.

And there was an arm-wrestling contest, which the gorilla won – but it was close!

Everyone enjoyed playing Ring the Rhinoceros…

...and the Giraffe Slide was very popular among the smaller animals.

Some of the animals felt homesick, and Noah tried to cheer them up.

He let the penguins take turns in the fridge…

…while the polar bears made the most of the small space available.

The parrots all wanted to sit on Noah's shoulder, but they had to take turns too.

He put out bowls of water for the wading birds, who were missing their shallow pools.

Animals like to keep clean, so Noah set up an Animal Cleaning Station.

The elephants got special treatment in return for spraying water.

The drying and body care team rubbed and scrubbed.

The trunk and tusk team dusted and polished.

The toenail specialist cleaned and brushed.

HOW'S THAT? O.K?

HOW DO YOU LIKE YOUR BODY RUB?

WHAT A PAMPERED CREATURE I AM!

Lar gibbon

Pygmy anteater

Crimson-breasted shrike

Leopard

There were some animals who only came out at night. To make them feel at home Noah made a special Nocturnal Room.

Everything was fine until somebody put the light on.

It was a frog and a rabbit – and that wasn't all they did. They tied the ring-tailed lemurs' tails together...

they bounced on a sleepy buffalo...

WHEEEE!

BLLLLL!

BLLLLL!

HOW RUDE!

and they made faces at the puma.

Noah was not pleased.

BEHAVE, OR ELSE!

OOOER...

SIGH

It seemed a shame not to make the most of the water, so Noah built a floating platform where the water-loving creatures could sit or go for a swim.

Noah even tried water-skiing, pulled by a friendly dolphin.

The elephant had a horrible sinking feeling but still enjoyed being pulled along by a small whale.

As if all this wasn't enough, Noah started a weekly
show in which everyone could take part.

There were competitions for the most unusual nose,
the strangest beak and the most interesting horns.

Some of the animals started a band –
Enrico Elephant and his Animal Stompers.
They got the whole Ark rocking.

A kookaburra and a hyena got together in a comedy double act. They laughed so much at their own jokes that they couldn't even finish them.

HA HA HA HA... YOU'LL LOVE THIS ONE! HA HA!...

Spotted hyena

Kookaburra

HERE'S A GOOD ONE, HA HA... THERE'S THIS GORILLA AND THIS RABBIT, IN A CLEARING RIGHT?... HA HA HA...

THAT'S RIGHT, AND THE RABBIT SAYS... NO, THE GORILLA SAYS... HA HA HA THE GORILLA SAYS...

HE SAYS "RABBIT" HE SAYS, HA HA HA, OH DEAR... "RABBIT" HE SAYS, HA HA...

HA HA HA I CAN'T GO ON, HA HA HA HA HA... HE SAYS...

They were terrible.

RUBBISH, AREN'T THEY?

Lynx

TOO RIGHT!

Meerkat

Eurasian badger

Sea otter

LAUGH? I DIDN'T!

Golden lion tamarin

I'VE SEEN HOLES IN THE GROUND FUNNIER THAN THEM!

Rabbit

The Bactrian camel and the dromedary did their Amazing Hump Trick.

And Noah and Japhet did a tap dance.
That went down a storm.

The animals were all having a lovely time.
But then there was a lurch and a crunch…

The flood had gone and the Ark was on dry land! Noah hastily got the animals together for a group photograph.

It was time for the animals to leave. Noah had taken good care of them but now they wanted to go back to their homes all over the world.

They all said their goodbyes and thank yous to Noah as he checked them off on his list, and they promised to keep in touch. Noah watched and waved as they disappeared over the horizon,
two by two
        by two
          by two
            by two
              by two…

Haartibeest

Lion

Zebra

Gorilla

Duck-billed platypus

Water opossum

Three-toed sloth

Striped skunk

Star-nosed mole

Pronghorn

Gaur

Lar gibbon

Guinea fowl

Sicklebill

Redshank

Great white pelican

New Guinea forest wallaby

Golden lion tamarin

Echidna

Pygmy anteater

Elephant shrew

Grey hamster

Anaconda

Robin